ELIZA'S FAITH

THE AMISH SISTERS BOOK 1

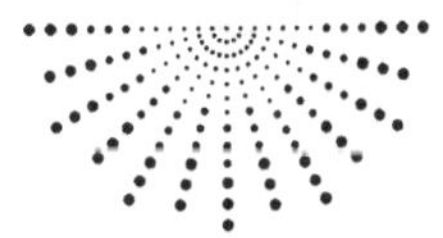

SARAH MILLER

SWEETBOOKHUB.COM

THE AMISH SISTERS

Welcome to my new book. It is one of three books about three Amish Sisters. Each book can be read alone but I'm sure you will love all of them.

We have:

Eliza's Faith

Patience's Faith

Annie's Faith

If you love Amish romance join my Newsletter. I will let you know as soon as my new books are available. You will also get occasional exclusive free books. You can join here

Blessings,

Sarah Miller

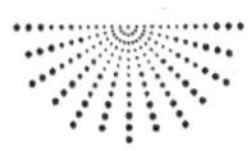

CHAPTER ONE

Faith's Creek, Pennsylvania.

"Do you think he'll be there?" Eliza Graber asked as she and her two sisters sat around the kitchen table.

It had been raining that afternoon and the Graber sisters, Annie, the eldest, Eliza, and their younger sister Patience, were busy with their needlework. Their mother, Barbara, took a batch of freshly baked rolls from the oven, filling the house with the scent of baking. She looked up and smiled, shaking her head.

"It hardly matters if he is or isn't, you'll never pluck

up the courage to speak to him," Annie said, laying down her needlework, as Patience giggled.

"I will," Eliza replied, hurt by her sister's lack of confidence in her.

"You could have spoken to him at the picnic last week." Annie raised her eyebrows.

"Or after the service last month. He was all on his own, just sitting alone," Patience continued.

Eliza sighed. Her sisters were right, of course, and she wondered whether she would ever have the courage to speak with Matthew Lloyd, their friend and neighbor, who also happened to be the man she was in love with. He had blossomed from a gangly boy into a strapping and handsome man, with dark blond hair and beautiful blue eyes. She was not the only woman in Faith's Creek who had fallen for him, and she had her doubts as to his feelings for her. Still, she could dream, though as Annie so often pointed out, a dream is nothing if you do not move towards it... if it had no hope of coming true.

"I'm sure your sister knows what she's doing," Barbara said, placing the rolls onto the cooling rack and dusting off her apron.

"She's going to be left on the shelf if she's not careful," Annie said, and Eliza laughed.

"You're the eldest, I don't see any signs of you finding a husband," she said, and Annie gave her a withering look.

"You know I don't intend to marry, I want to be a schoolteacher and I can't do that if I'm chasing after husbands now, can I?" she said.

Eliza smiled. She had always liked teasing her elder sister, who, in truth, could wed any man she wished. She was beautiful, with dark brown hair and hazel eyes, a soft complexion, and rosy cheeks, and Eliza knew that any number of young men in Faith's Creek would be happy to make their proposal to her.

"Oh, do speak to him, Eliza, you must. Tonight's the perfect opportunity," Patience said, putting her hand on Eliza's and smiling.

"You're such a romantic, Patience. You think that just because I speak to Matthew, there'll be a wedding next week," Eliza replied, and her younger sister laughed.

"I just want you to be happy, is that so awful? He's

perfect for you, The two of you have been friends for so long, wouldn't it just be wonderful if you got married," Patience said, appearing misty-eyed, as though caught up in her own fantasy.

"It has its attractions," Eliza admitted, glancing at the clock on the kitchen wall.

"We'd better get ready, you know what they're like, board games wait for no man, or woman," Annie said.

The three sisters rose to their feet. They were to attend a board games evening at a local farm, where there was a barn big enough for all the town's young people to come together. It was organized by Bishop Amos Beiler and the three sisters had been looking forward to it ever since the announcement had been made at service last month.

"Go and wash your faces and get ready," their *mamm* said, smiling at the three of them, as Patience and Annie clattered up the stairs from the kitchen.

"Should I speak with him *Mamm?*" Eliza asked, and her mother smiled.

"You should do what you think is right, Eliza.

Matthew Lloyd is a good man, His parents have always been good friends and neighbors to us and I'm sure he'd make a good husband for you, though I don't always agree with women making the first move. You might wait and see what he has to say for himself first."

Eliza nodded. "I'll try not to get too caught up in the idea," she said, but her *mamm* shook her head.

"There's no harm in dreaming, Eliza. Hurry now, or you'll be late," Barbara said.

With a smile, Eliza made her way upstairs.

Patience had just finished in the bathroom and now Eliza splashed water on her face and lathered up the soap, gazing at herself for a moment in the mirror. She had always thought her elder sister to be the prettiest woman she knew, though Patience, with her blonde hair and blue eyes, was fast blossoming too. Eliza was something of them both, with light brown hair and similarly colored eyes. She washed the soap from her face and dried it with a rough towel, before putting on her kapp and joining her sisters on the landing.

"Ready?" Annie asked, and Eliza nodded.

They made their way back downstairs, where their *daed*, Samuel, had just come in from feeding the chickens in the yard. The girls lived with their parents on a small homestead on the edge of town, the family's home for three generations. It was a happy life and one which Eliza had come to cherish, even if her Rumspringa had shown her more of the world than she might have imagined.

"Look at you three, aren't you a picture," Samuel said, and all three girls smiled.

"Are you walking them over to Jackson's farm?" Barbara asked, and their *daed* nodded.

"It's a nice evening, I might even call on Bishop Beiler on my way back," he said.

"You three enjoy yourselves, now," Barbara said, kissing each of them on the cheek.

"We will," Patience replied.

"And remember what I said," Barbara said, turning to Eliza, who blushed.

"What did Mamm say to you?" Annie asked as soon as they were outside.

"Now then, I don't want any tittle-tattle," Samuel said, as Patience took him by the arm.

"Eliza's going to speak with Matthew Lloyd tonight," she said, and their *daed* raised an eyebrow.

"Is that so?" he asked, causing Eliza to blush.

She hated to think that her *daed* might be displeased with her. She cared about what he thought and so far, she had kept the subject of marriage a close secret, confiding in no one but her *mamm* as to her true feelings, though they were plain to see.

"I like him," she admitted.

"He's a *gut* man, he comes from a *gut* family. I wouldn't stand against it, though I'd have preferred it if you'd asked me first. I've never been strict with you girls, but when it comes to my daughters, I like to know what's going on," he said, giving Eliza a firm look.

"He probably won't even be there and if he is, I doubt he'll feel the same. He'll say we're just friends or something like that," Eliza sighed, wishing she had never even mentioned it.

Her feelings for Matthew were clear, but what was

also clear was that a dozen other women in Faith's Creek would happily have that same conversation with him. She might be in love with him, but that was no reason for him to be in love with her. With her nerves rising, Eliza lagged behind the others, her heart beating fast at the prospect of what was to come.

"It's good of you to walk us *Daed*," Annie said, as they came to the track leading up to Jackson's farm, where the game night was to take place in one of the barns.

"Nonsense, I'm happy to, and I'll come to walk you home later on," he said, smiling, as he kissed all three of them goodbye.

"Give our regards to Bishop Beiler," Annie called out, and their father waved his hand.

"Enjoy yourselves," he said, as the three sisters walked arm in arm up the track toward the farm.

Eliza wondered if she should go home, surely this was going to be a disaster?

The sun was beginning to set and the barn was lit by lamps, making the place look homey and welcoming. Already a dozen or so of their friends and acquaintances had gathered. Haybales had been positioned around the barn, with chess sets and draught boards laid out on each, and at the far end was a low trestle table, covered in all manner of good things to eat.

"Doesn't it look lovely," Patience said, waving to several of her friends, who came hurrying over.

"I'm sure I'm getting too old for this, if I keep coming to these things I'll soon be teaching half of them," Annie said, as she and Eliza watched Patience be made a fuss of by her friends.

"You enjoy it really, I know you do," Eliza said, turning to her sister, who raised her eyebrows.

"Well, I enjoy beating you all at chess, though I shouldn't be so proud," she said with a wink.

Eliza laughed. "You've got a talent, use it, don't hide your lamp under a bushel, that's what the Bible says," Eliza said, and now it was Annie's turn to laugh.

"It also says a lot about vanity and pride. Anyway, have you seen him yet?" she asked, glancing around.

Eliza looked too, though she could see no sign of Matthew, nor any of the young men he hung out with. She was just about to sit down at one of the haybales and challenge Annie to a game of draughts when voices along the track caused her to turn. She knew Matthew's voice, even without seeing him, and he was calling out a greeting to Mr. Jackson's son, Marlin.

With a smile, she turned, ready to greet him, but the smile soon fell from her face and she let out an anguished gasp. There was Matthew, entering the barn, a smile on his face, but on his arm, was Betty Lapp, the sight of which brought a tear to her eye. She clutched at Annie, who sighed and shook her head, as Betty waved to them, a look of pride on her face. Betty Lapp was a stunning beauty, one who could have her choice of any man she wished and by the looks of it, she had chosen Matthew ...

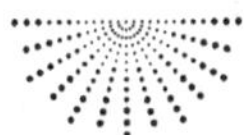

Eliza fought back the tears. Until now, she had no inclination that Matthew and Betty were a couple and the sight of the two of them together was almost too much to bear. She had spent so long building herself up to this moment, imagining what it would be and what words she would speak, that now she felt entirely deflated. It was as though her dreams had been shattered. Swallowing down her tears she turned forlornly to Annie, shaking her head and sighing.

"Oh, Eliza, I'm sorry. I never imagined he'd be with someone else," Annie said, putting her arm around her shoulders.

"I should have guessed. I've dithered over this for too

long. How can you expect someone to wait for you if they don't even know they're supposed to be waiting?" she said.

Annie shook her head. "But still, Betty Lapp of all women. She's a terrible flirt, you've heard what *Mamm* says about her. I can't imagine why Matthew would be interested in her, it's astonishing."

Eliza glanced over again to where Matthew and Betty were talking animatedly with several others. Patience was already absorbed in a board game and she had paid no attention to the new arrivals. The barn buzzed with happiness, filled with young people calling out greetings and settling down to play the games. No one but Annie understood how alone she felt.

"Do you think they're together?" Eliza asked.

Annie pondered for a moment. "Well, you know what Betty's like, she might just have met him on the track up here and took his arm. She's that sort of woman," she said, a disapproving tone entering her voice.

"Oh, I don't feel like this anymore," Eliza said,

pushing aside the draught pieces and rising to her feet.

"Are you going to let a little thing like this spoil your evening? He hasn't even said 'hello' yet, and you've not spoken a word to him. Come on, Eliza, you've got more fight in you than that. Isn't it Matthew that you're in love with? You can't just quit now, you've not even asked him," Annie said, taking Eliza by the arm.

"But what if he says no, what if I spoil our friendship?" she asked.

Annie smiled. "No one said it was easy. If you want a husband, you'll have to work for it. Isn't that how it works? I don't know, Eliza, you give up too easily sometimes. If you want something, you've got to grasp it with both hands. That's what I think about teaching. If I want to be a schoolteacher and do my best for this community, then I've got to work for it. It's the same for you, husbands don't just grow on trees waiting to be plucked like a ripe piece of fruit. You've got to cultivate the relationship and you've certainly got to do more than give up when the expected rain doesn't come," she said, but Eliza was not entirely listening, watching instead, as Matthew caught her eye and waved.

He really was the most handsome man in the room. Eliza knew that others thought it too, the looks of other women were following him, as he and Betty sat down to play at one of the hay bales. Just then, Patience came hurrying over, a plate of food in her hand, she plopped down next to Eliza and Annie, smiling at them, oblivious to what was happening.

"I won, can you believe it, I won? I checkmated Esther in a dozen moves," she said.

Annie raised her eyebrow. "Even chess is an occasion for sin, Patience. Less pride and more humility," she said.

Patience rolled her eyes. "It's only a game, Annie. Anyway, is he here yet?" she asked, turning to Eliza.

With a heavy heart, Eliza pointed across the room to where Matthew and Betty sat playing draughts. Though she was dressed modestly, her kapp on her head, there was little of modesty in Betty's demeanor. She was like the cat that had got the cream, her eyes fixed on Matthew, and a look of triumph on her face.

"He's here," Eliza said, and Patience gasped.

"Oh..." she began.

"Oh, indeed," Eliza said, shaking her head and turning back to the draught board.

"I told you, don't let it get to you. Why don't you have something to eat," Annie said, but Eliza shook her head.

Any enthusiasm she had had for the evening was now gone, replaced only with the desire to no longer endure the sight of Betty Lapp lauding it over every other woman in the barn. She rose to her feet and dusted herself off, ready to walk home alone, if her sisters would not accompany her.

"Where are you going?" Patience hissed.

"Home, I can't stand this any longer," Eliza replied, but both her sisters now pulled her back down to the bale.

"If you leave now, you'll regret it," Patience said, and Annie nodded.

"Wise words, Patience is right. If you don't speak with him, you'll regret it for the rest of your life.

You'll never be happy because you'll always be wondering what would have happened if you'd just spoken to him. There's no harm in saying 'hello' is there? He's probably sitting there wondering why his oldest friend hasn't come over to speak to him," she said, giving Eliza such a withering look that she began to giggle.

"All right, I suppose so," she said, with a reluctant sigh.

"We know so," Patience said, pointing toward Matthew and Betty.

Eliza got to her feet again, though now her heart was racing fast at the prospect of what she was about to do. She was naturally a modest and somewhat retiring type, her two sisters being possessed of the greater confidence. But whilst Eliza had not the outward signs of fearlessness, she was possessed of inner courage, which now seemed to take over.

As she approached the haybale, where Matthew and Betty were playing draughts, the two of them looked up and a smile came over Matthew's face. Eliza glanced behind her, to find Annie and Patience watching her intently, urging her on by their looks.

She smiled at Matthew, her hands clasped tightly together, as she summoned all her nerves.

"I'm not interrupting you, am I?" she asked.

Betty laughed. "Not at all, Eliza, how nice to see you. I haven't seen you in ages, not since the last service. Have you been hiding?" she asked, fluttering her eyelashes at Eliza, the tone of her voice sounding forced, as though she were trying her best to be polite.

"Oh, there's been a lot of work to see to on the homestead. You know what it's like at this time of year, my *mamm* and I have been busy planting and then I help *Daed* with the animals too," she said.

Betty nodded and pretended she was interested but her smile was more like a smirk and missed her eyes. "It must be so busy for you, my *mamm* and *daed* don't expect me to help like that, not if I'm going to leave Faith's Creek for the city," she said, glancing at Matthew.

"Actually, I was just wondering if we might talk for a moment," Eliza said, turning to Matthew, who seemed surprised but pleased at the suggestion.

"Sure thing, I'm sure Betty can find someone else to play draughts with for a few moments," he said.

Betty forced her face into an ungracious smile. "You bring him back to me, you hear," she called out, as Matthew rose to his feet and he and Eliza made their way through the crowd.

The evening was still warm, though the sun had set, the moon rising on the horizon to take its place in the starry sky above. They left behind the hustle and bustle of the barn, leaning on a gate that led into one of the cornfields. The air was cool and the swaying sheathes seemed to stretch endlessly out across the landscape beyond.

"She's certainly got you on a leash," Eliza said, grinning at Matthew, who shook his head.

"Who? Betty? Oh, she just caught me on the way up here, I've not been able to get away from her. She's a nice enough girl but..." he began, his words trailing off.

"But she's a flirt. I don't think there's a man in Faith's Creek she hasn't been on the arm of at some point or another," Eliza said.

Now that she was alone with Matthew, her confidence had returned. They had known one another since they were children before either of them could remember. But it was only in recent months that her feelings for him had changed. Perhaps they had both grown up, for Eliza was confident in knowing what she wanted. Unlike her sister, she had no desire to teach and she certainly had no thoughts of making her way to the city and leaving Faith's Creek behind.

Eliza loved the way of life here and the thought of leaving it all behind was painful. She wanted to be like her *mamm*, to work on a homestead and raise *kinner*, to live the kind of life she knew had made so many others happy and she wanted to live it with Matthew. Now, she turned to him, summoning all her courage, and readying herself to speak. She had rehearsed these words so often in the past few days, like an actor learning lines for a play. But just as she was about to speak, he began to laugh.

"You've certainly got an opinion of her," he said, shaking his head.

"But what's so funny?" she demanded, for she had not expected him to respond in such a way.

"I'm sorry. It's just that... well, I was hoping you'd come over and I wondered why you didn't. I wanted a reason to speak with you too, there's been something playing on my mind, something I need to tell you," he said, smiling at her and taking her by the hand.

Eliza's heart leaped into her throat and seemed to wedge there, what was he going to say?

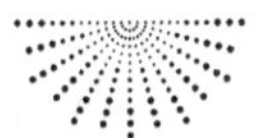

CHAPTER THREE

Eliza was surprised by his actions, she had not expected him to be so forward. Her heart was now racing like a runaway horse, as he held her by the hand and gazed into her eyes. For a moment, she was lost for words, unable to recall anything of the script she had prepared or the practice she had undertaken. He had floored her and now she wondered what it was he wanted to say.

"I... I don't understand ..." she began, but he shook his head.

"I'm just glad to be away from Betty and with you," he said.

Eliza swallowed hard.

"You... you are?" she asked, and he nodded.

"It's all I've thought about. I wanted to speak with you as soon as I got here, but I just couldn't get away from her. I was hoping she might find someone else to speak with, but she's clung to me like a limpet all evening. I'm just glad it was you that rescued me"

At these words, Eliza felt her heart skip a beat and she wondered if he too felt as she did. She could hear Annie's words about the blossoming of the tree and the risk that was worth it and she smiled at him, determined now to tell him the feelings in her heart.

"I have to say, I was wondering..." she began, trying to choose her words carefully, "I wasn't sure if you were here with Betty because... well... because you... you liked her."

"Like her? I don't dislike anybody, it's not in my nature, but 'like' her? Oh, no, not like that. Besides, you should know, shouldn't you?" he said.

Eliza looked at him with confusion. This had all seemed so simple in her mind. She would speak to Matthew and tell him how she felt, he would respond and that would be that. But now she felt entirely confused by his words, as though he were speaking in riddles, riddles she could not understand.

"I should know what?" she asked, his hand still grasped in hers.

"That it's you I like. It's you I've always liked, I've been in love with you since I was in dungarees, can't you tell?" he said.

Eliza gasped, almost falling back against the gate in her shock. "But that's what I wanted to talk to you about. That's what I wanted to tell you. I feel just the same," she replied, and he shook his head and laughed.

"You mean to say we've both danced around one another like a couple of chickens, each too nervous to speak to the other? You know, I've worried about tonight for weeks. I said to myself, 'Matthew, you've just got to come out and say it,' but I couldn't do it, I didn't want to lose you as a friend and I didn't know if you felt the same," he said, and she laughed.

"That's just how I've felt too. I didn't know if you liked me or not, or what you'd say if I told you. I just knew I was in love with you..." she said, gazing up into his eyes.

This was more than she had ever imagined, the feelings hidden for so many years now expressed. It felt like a pressure cooker letting off steam, the two of them shaking their heads in disbelief.

"I don't know why I was so worried. I just thought you couldn't ever feel like this. We've been friends for so long and sometimes, when two people are friends, they can't be something more. It just doesn't work and..." he began, his words suddenly trailing off, as he looked at her and smiled.

"It's all right, now we know, isn't that all that matters. We're both as bad as one another, I couldn't tell you and you couldn't tell me. I was so worried when I saw you with Betty, I was all set to run home. It was Annie who stopped me,, She said I would be a fool if I did and Patience told me I'd regret it the rest of my life," Eliza admitted.

"And you don't regret it now?" he asked.

She shook her head feeling tears of joy welling in her eyes. "All I feel is relief and joy," she replied.

Just then, half a dozen others came up the track, calling out greetings and apologies for being late. Matthew quickly removed his hand from Eliza's, the two of them leaning on the gate and looking out over the moonlit cornfield.

"Do you want to tell people?" Matthew asked when the newcomers had gone into the barn.

"What would I be telling them? That the two of us had found the courage to talk?" she asked.

He shook his head. "Eliza, it's not just telling you how I feel that's put the fear of *Gott* into me, it's something else too, a question I've got to ask you," he said, and Eliza's heart skipped another beat.

It was one thing to tell him that she loved him, but quite another to know what to do next. She had thought about this too, imagining what it would be for him to ask the question he now seemed intent on doing. Eliza knew what her answer would be, and she smiled at him, as he glanced nervously around, before dropping to one knee.

"Oh goodness," she gasped, as he took hold of her hand and gazed up at her.

"I don't want to waste any more time, Eliza. I love you and I want to ask you to marry me, that's what's been on my heart all this time. I've been so nervous, but I was determined to do it tonight, whatever you might have said. I'm sorry you got the wrong idea about Betty and I sure am glad you had the courage to come and speak to me."

"I wanted to," she said, and he brought her hand to his lips.

"Will you marry me, Eliza? That's what I want to know. I'm so in love with you, I couldn't keep it inside me if I tried," he said, and she gasped, her heart racing and her hands trembling.

In a moment, a dozen feelings rushed through her, so unprepared had she been for such a thing to happen. When she had left home that night, she had thought of sharing her feelings with Matthew, perhaps even discovering that he shared them, too. But to now be asked this question, to find him knelt before her, and to know that she wanted nothing else in all the world but this, filled her heart with joy.

"Of course I'll marry you, there's nothing I want more than to marry you," she said, as he let out a sigh of relief and bowed his head.

It was as though the pressure cooker had let off its steam, the two of them now looking at one another and laughing, as he rose to his feet and flung his arms around her.

"You don't know how happy I am to hear that," he said, and he kissed her on the cheek, blushing, as he stepped back and glanced back toward the barn in case they had been seen.

"If it's anything like I'm feeling then I'm glad," she replied, slipping her hand into his, "though poor Betty might not be so pleased."

"She's got a string of suitors from here to Bird-In-Hand, she'll not be too worried. But we should keep this to ourselves, for now, you know the tradition. Let's wait until the summer comes, then we'll tell everyone," he said, and she nodded.

Eliza knew she would find it hard to contain her excitement. She wanted to run back into the barn and shout it at the top of her voice. Annie and Patience would be pleased. They would want to celebrate, but Eliza liked the idea of tradition and the thought of keeping a secret with Matthew was exciting.

"Do you think they'll be happy?" she asked.

Matthew nodded. "Why wouldn't they be? We're perfect for one another and even if they think not, I do. You're the only one I've ever wanted, right back when we were children I knew it. I even told my *mamm* once, '*Mamm*,' I said, 'I'm going to marry Eliza Graber,' and now I will," he said, shaking his head and laughing.

"And what did she say?" Eliza asked for she knew how protective Louisa Lloyd was of her son.

"She said, we'd have to see about that. But she didn't say *nee*. I know you'll make a wonderful *fraa* and I just hope I'll make an adequate husband," he said.

Eliza smiled. She knew that Matthew would make the very best of husbands. He had always been such a kind and considerate man, even in their childhood, she had seen such traits in him. The day he had dived into the creek to rescue her on a hot summer's day when she had fallen off the swing and the time he had carried her on his back all the way from the woods on the edge of the town when she had fallen and sprained her ankle.

It was memories such as these that had made her so ready to say *jah* to his question, a response which had seemed as natural to her as the feelings she had now come to possess in her heart. Eliza was in love and the thought of marrying Matthew made her feel happier than anything ever had before, a happiness which it was clear he shared, too. Now, they smiled at one another, just as a shout came from the door of the barn.

"Aren't you coming to play, Matthew? There's a chess set with your name on it here," one of the other boys called out.

"We'd better go back, don't you think? They'll be wondering where we've got to. Let's keep it a secret," he said, and the two of them hurried back to the barn, where the board games evening was in full swing.

"Where have you been?" Betty asked, an indignant look on her face, as Eliza and Matthew returned to her side.

"Oh, it just got a little stuffy in here, that's all," Matthew said, glancing at Eliza.

"I'd better go and sit with my sisters, they'll wonder where I've got to," Eliza said, and blushing, she smiled at Matthew, before returning across the barn to where Annie and Patience were busy playing draughts.

"Well, what did he say?" Annie asked as the two sisters looked up expectantly.

Eliza nodded, hoping that somehow, she could contain the excitement which had built up inside her. She wanted to shout it from the rooftops, to tell everybody how in love she was. But instead, she smoothed down her dress and sat down primly next to Patience, looking down at the board and smiling.

"I think he made it clear what his next move would be," she said, and both her sisters let out a cry of delight.

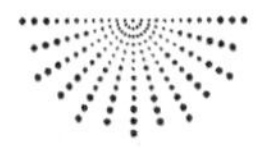

CHAPTER FOUR

It was two months later, and summer was at its height in Faith's Creek. The days were long and warm, the evenings sultry and sticky. These were hot, lazy days, when lemonade was drunk on porches and only the children seemed to summon the energy for anything but sitting out and talking in the shade. Eliza had been busy helping her *mamm* and *daed* around the smallholding, seeing to the animals, and working in the vegetable patch and garden. Annie was busy with her studies and Patience was at that age when she shunned helping about the house, spending her days instead with books or crochet.

But Eliza still kept her secret even though the urge to

reveal it was growing stronger by the day. After the proposal at the board games evening, she and Matthew had agreed to keep their engagement a secret, though they had visited Bishop Beiler and his *fraa* Sarah to share the good news. The Bishop had made a point of telling them to share it with their families just as soon as summer came and that was what they intended to do. Today was the day they had planned to sit down with their families and tell them, a day for which Eliza was both excited for and terrified at the prospect.

She knew that her sisters would be thrilled, in fact, she was almost certain that they had guessed. How could they not have noticed the look in her eyes and the smile on her face? Her *mamm* too had behaved differently with her, as though she too was expecting a revelation to come soon. But it was Matthew that she worried about. He was an only child and his *mamm* doted on him to the point of distraction. Would she be happy with his choice of bride? Eliza had tried her best to be the very model of what was expected, but still, she had her doubts as to whether Louisa Lloyd would accept her.

"Matthew and his parents are going to call round

later," Eliza said, as she entered the kitchen carrying a basket of vegetables from the garden.

"Is that so? I wasn't expecting them," her *mamm* said, raising her eyebrows, a knowing look coming over her face.

"They're our neighbors and you're always saying how important it is to be hospitable to others. I thought we could all have cake and coffee together, or some lemonade in this heat, I'll bake," Eliza replied, trying to sound as casual as she possibly could.

"Since when have you volunteered to bake? It's Patience who does that. But all right, if you want to. It'll be nice to see them, I'm sure you and Matthew have got lots to say," her *mamm* said, as Eliza turned red as the beets she had in her basket.

Her mamm left her alone in the kitchen and she took out flour, sugar, and eggs, intending to bake a sponge in the hope of showing Louisa she would make a suitable wife. As she was mixing up the batter, Annie came clattering down the stairs, a pile of books under her arm and she stopped short at the sight of Eliza with her sleeves rolled up, shaking her head, and laughing.

"Now I really have seen it all. Eliza baking a cake. What's that all about?" she asked.

"Matthew and his parents are coming over this afternoon, I thought it would be nice for us all to get together. Will you be here?" she asked, mixing currants and raisins through the batter, and spooning it into a tin.

"Is there something you've got to tell us?" Annie asked, looking pointedly at Eliza and smiling.

"You'd better be here to see, I suppose," Eliza said, and her sister nodded.

"I'll be there if only to see if you can bake," she said, and she made her way outside to read in the sunshine.

Eliza smiled to herself, she was looking forward to the surprise, even if it was really to be no surprise at all.

Matthew and his parents – Louisa and Isaac – arrived promptly at four o'clock. Mr. Lloyd was a homesteader, like Eliza's father, and the two men had much in common, not least the length of their beards. Eliza's mother and Louisa had been friends for many years, and they greeted one another like sisters, falling into the usual manner of gossip which women of their generation were want to do. Patience had been summoned from her room and Annie had come inside from her reading so that the whole family was now gathered around the kitchen table.

Eliza proudly placed the cake she had baked in the center of the table, along with a jug of lemonade, for it had been decided that it was too hot for coffee. She had smiled at Matthew, who had remained quiet, as though he too were nervous about what was to come, the two of them had decided that it would be he who would make the announcement. Eliza was desperate for her family to know how happy she was, she wanted the whole of Faith's Creek to know and to share in their good news.

"Well, isn't this lovely," Barbara said, as they sat down to the cake, "I've never known Eliza offer to bake before, but you've certainly done well, this cake is delicious, so moist and fruity."

"It's an excellent cake," Louisa said, smiling at Eliza, who blushed.

It was Louisa who she had wanted to impress, and this accolade gave her further confidence in what was to come. She glanced at Matthew, who had just taken a big bite of cake, before clearing her throat to address them.

"I'm glad we could all get together. We don't do this enough, you're our neighbors and it's so nice to have you here," she said, and Matthew's parents laughed.

"And we're glad you're our neighbors, Eliza, we truly are," Mr. Lloyd said, "especially with a cake like this."

"Actually, *Daed, Mamm,* there's something we wanted to tell you all," Matthew said, having taken a drink of lemonade and a deep breath.

Eliza glanced at Annie, who smiled at her, and Patience pricked up her ears, all eyes now on Matthew, who seemed even more nervous than before.

"What is it, Matthew?" Louisa asked, looking puzzled.

"Well, Eliza and I have some happy news to share with you all. We've been keeping it a secret these past few months, though perhaps some of you have guessed," he said, glancing at Annie, who nodded.

"Well, a sister can't keep a secret from another sister," she said, and Matthew laughed.

"I guess not. But we wanted to do things properly and I know that summer's the time for such things," he said, and Eliza watched as Louisa's expression changed.

"What are you saying, Matthew?" she asked, and Matthew smiled.

"Eliza and I are getting married, *Mamm*, I asked her back in May and she was *gut* enough to say *jah*," he said, reaching out and taking Eliza by the hand.

"Oh, what wonderful news, oh, we're so happy for you," Barbara said, leaping to her feet and hurrying to embrace her daughter, as her *daed* too offered his congratulations.

"You have my blessing, both of you. You'll make a

good marriage, I'm certain of it," he said, leaning over the table to shake Matthew by the hand.

"Thank you, sir, thank you, Mrs. Graber. I promise you I'll take good care of Eliza, I'll be the best husband I can be," Matthew said, and Samuel laughed.

"I'm sure you will, she's chosen well," he replied.

Annie and Patience had leaped to their feet in excitement and embraced Eliza, talk already turning to the wedding and what a happy day it would be.

"We can help make your dress," Patience said.

"And walk with you into the church, I can pick posies of flowers up in the woods if the wedding is to be soon, that is," Annie said, and Eliza laughed.

"We haven't really thought about it," she said, turning to Matthew, who shrugged.

"I just want us to be married, that's all. It doesn't matter if it's in a barn or out front here. We just need Bishop Beiler and a prayer book, I love Eliza and I just want to marry her," Matthew said.

"We're so pleased for you both, aren't we, Louisa?"

Matthew's father said, but Eliza was surprised to now see Louisa rise from the table, her face ashen and her hands trembling.

"Would you excuse me for a moment, I need to take a little air," she said, hurrying to the door.

"Louisa, are you all right?" Barbara called after her, but the door had slammed shut, and the others looked around them in surprise.

"Is she all right?" Eliza asked, glancing at Matthew, who had a puzzled look on his face.

"I'd better go and see. Perhaps she's just feeling a little under the weather," Matthew replied, rising to his feet.

But Eliza caught his arm, as she too rose, the others all questioning Louisa's strange behavior.

"I'll go, you stay here and cut some more cake. It'll be all right," she said, and before Matthew could reply, Eliza followed Louisa out onto the porch.

Louisa was standing leaning on the rail, her head bowed, and her shoulders hunched, as though she were crying. Eliza could not help but feel sorry for her, wondering what it was that was wrong. Had she done something to upset her? She had looked so sorrowful at the news, news which was meant to be happy for them all.

"Oh, Eliza," Louisa said, turning at the sound of Eliza's footsteps and pulling a delicate lace handkerchief from her sleeve.

"Are you all right? What's wrong Mrs. Lloyd? Have we done something to upset you?" Eliza asked, as Louisa wiped her eyes and forced a smile across her face.

"*Nee*... it's not that..." she began, as Eliza stepped forward and put her hand on Louisa's shoulder.

"Listen, I promise I'll be a good *fraa* to Matthew. I really do love him and he loves me. I know it's come as a shock, but we've had these feelings for one another for as long as each of us could remember. It's just taken a while to realize them, that's all. We thought we were doing the right thing to wait until summer, just like the tradition," Eliza said, still trying to understand why Louisa should be so upset.

Did she bear some grudge against Eliza? She wracked her brains, wondering what she might have done to offend the woman who was soon to be her mother-in-law. Eliza had always thought that she and Louisa got on well, for certainly, her mother was on the friendliest of terms with her. It saddened Eliza to think that she had made some mistake or caused Louisa upset.

"Oh, Eliza. I don't doubt that you and Matthew are just right for one another. You're a *gut* girl, you always have been, and you know how fond I am of you. It's just... well, it's going to take me a while to get used to the thought of losing Matthew. He's my only son and... well, I'm probably far too overprotective of him, but that's my prerogative. I love him and I don't want to lose him," she said, beginning to cry once more.

Eliza breathed a sigh of relief. She had imagined herself to have done some terrible wrong and caused offense where she had never thought it to be found. She could understand Louisa's reluctance to let go of her son. It was surely the same for any mother and Eliza knew that Matthew had always been close to his mother. She took hold of Louisa's hand and squeezed it, wanting only to comfort and reassure her.

"You're not losing him, I promise you that. I'm not

going to take him away or stop you from seeing him. I want you and his *daed* to be just as much a part of our family as my *mamm* and *daed*. We can all be one big family, that's what happens, isn't it? Didn't you feel the same when you married Mr. Lloyd?" she asked.

Louisa nodded through her tears. "I suppose so... oh, I'm just being silly, aren't I? The way I'm talking you'd think the two of you had just announced you were moving to California or something."

"I know it's a big change, it is for us, too. I've been nervous about this day for weeks, ever since Matthew asked me to marry him. I wanted to shout it from the rooftops, but I was worried about what everyone would think," Eliza said.

"And I've done nothing to make that better," Louisa replied, glancing at Eliza before turning away as though she was embarrassed.

Eliza was at a loss as to what to say. She wanted to reassure Louisa and make her understand that she had no intention of taking Matthew away. She wanted to stay in Faith's Creek and raise a family, surrounded by the family that she relied on so much and Louisa and Isaac would be just as much a part of that as her own *mamm* and *daed.*

She was about to reply when a call came across the fence and she looked up to find Bishop Amos Beiler and his *fraa* Sarah approaching. Eliza breathed a sigh of relief, as Louisa wiped her eyes, evidently not wishing for the Bishop to see the tears. Amos and Sarah made their way through the gate and Eliza went to meet them, glad to have visitors to distract from the awkward situation which had just unfolded.

"It's *gut* to see you, Eliza, you're looking happy," Sarah said, smiling at Eliza, who at that moment did not think she was looking particularly happy at all.

"Have you told them yet?" Amos asked, lowering his voice, but at that moment, Eliza's parents came hurrying from the house, calling out the *gut* news.

"We've got something wonderful to tell you, Amos, Sarah," Barbara called out.

"Is that right, Mrs. Graber?" he replied, feigning a look of surprise.

"Eliza and Matthew Lloyd are to be married, he

proposed to her back in May and we've just found out this afternoon," Samuel said, and the Bishop made to congratulate Eliza on her happy news.

The party now returned inside and there was just enough cake to go round, as fresh glasses of lemonade were poured, and a toast was made to the happy couple. But Eliza could not help but watch Louisa who, though she forced a smile, still seemed distant and upset. It saddened Eliza to see it and put a damper on the celebrations, a day she had looked forward to ever since that night when Matthew had asked her to marry him.

"Will your *mamm* be all right?" Eliza asked Matthew, as later on that evening they bid one another goodbye.

"She'll come round to the idea. It's just a shock for her at the moment. I don't know why... she knew that one day I'd get married. Perhaps she just wasn't expecting it so soon. Don't worry about it, though. It's not like I'm running off to the big city and marrying a girl she's never met before. She loves you like her own, she'll come round. Well, goodnight," he said, and kissed her on the cheek, before hurrying down the porch steps after his parents.

But Eliza did worry and later that evening, when her *mamm* and *daed* were in bed, Eliza sat up with Annie and told her what Louisa had said.

"You don't need to worry about that. It's natural for parents to feel like that about their children. I've been reading about it, actually. They call it 'stages of development,' so for example, take the first day of school for a child. That's a big step for any parent, suddenly they're letting their child go for the first time and some can't handle it. They get upset, but usually, it's the child who makes the break," Annie said, with an air of learning.

"But Matthew's twenty years old, it's not like that at all," Eliza replied, but her sister shook her head.

"It's precisely like that, all the books on teaching talk about it. She doesn't want to let go. It doesn't matter if he's twenty or five, a parent's instinct is still the same. Don't take it personally. She would feel precisely the same whoever you were. It'll be all right in the end. He wants to marry you and you want to marry him. That's all that matters," Annie said, closing her textbooks and bidding Eliza goodnight.

Eliza sat for an hour or so in the kitchen, the last

remnants of the cake lying in the middle of the table. She felt confused as to Louisa's feelings toward her and she offered up a silent prayer in the hope of resolution. In it, she asked *Gott* to bless their union and to find a way through Louisa's sadness so that come their wedding day all might be well. She wanted to be liked and she wanted Louisa to accept her as a daughter-in-law. She had no desire to take Matthew away and it was with those thoughts in mind that she made her way to bed, her heart feeling heavy at the prospect of a problem still to be resolved.

As the summer came to an end, plans for the wedding were afoot, though Louisa still remained distant. Eliza did her best to be a friend to her, hoping to show through sheer determination that she could be a good daughter-in-law to Matthew's mother. But still, a shadow seemed to hang over the betrothal and Eliza was uncertain where she stood. She wanted so much to marry Matthew and be happy. The two of them often took walks together imagining their future.

It was a warm day, a gentle breeze blew across the cornfields and the sky was wide and blue, with not a cloud to be seen on the horizon. Eliza and Matthew walked together through the woodlands down by the creek. The waters were low and meandering at their side. They had enjoyed a picnic that afternoon with Annie and Patience and now Matthew had asked her to walk with him so that he might show her something special he had in mind.

"You know I don't like surprises," she said, smiling at him.

He laughed. "And neither do I, but you were going to spring one on me back in May, weren't you?" he said.

"But you sprung the bigger one. Come on, what's this now?" she asked, as he took hold of her hand.

"Just a little further and then you'll see," he said, leading her up a little path which brought them from the edge of the creek to a plot of land at the end of a track, her family homestead was just visible in the distance.

"Are we there? I don't see much," she said, looking around her.

A meadow, freshly mown, was surrounded by trees, the track giving up by a gate, through which Matthew now led her. There was the scent of freshly cut flowers in the air and a bird was sitting in a tree and singing its heart out, as though proud to perform for them on that late summer afternoon.

"You don't see much yet, but this is where we're going to live. Mr. Jackson sold it to my *daed* last week and he's given it over to me. I'm going to build you a house here, Eliza, a beautiful little house and maybe even a barn. Look, we can grow vegetables here and over there I'll plant an orchard, too," he said, leading her across the plot and pointing out this and that along the way.

Eliza was soon caught up in the idea and the two of them talked enthusiastically of all that might be.

"We could have twice as many hens as my parents have. I could sell the eggs," she said, and Matthew nodded.

"We can have all sorts of animals, a pig, and a cow. We'll have everything we need. I know it doesn't look like much yet, but I'll soon have it started," he said.

Eliza could not help but be taken up by his enthusiasm. "You used to just be a shy, clumsy boy who made me laugh with your antics," she said, as he put his arms around her.

"And now I'm still fooling around, but... well, I want you to be happy," he said, smiling down at her.

"I will be, so long as I've got you there with me," she said, and he smiled.

"We'd better get going, I told *Mamm* I'd be back for dinner early this evening. You're invited, too," he said, but Eliza shook her head.

She was still nervous about being around Mrs. Lloyd, as much as she had tried to be her friend. It was as though she was always under scrutiny, never able to be herself in the company of the woman who should have been such a support to her.

"I think I'll just go home," Eliza said, but Matthew insisted.

"I think she wants to speak to you, she's been doing a lot of thinking lately and I really think she's coming around to the idea of us being together. Will you give her a chance?" he asked.

Eliza felt guilty for being so judgmental and reluctantly she nodded and took Matthew by the arm. It was only a short walk to the house belonging to his parents, so close in fact that if they were to build their house on the plot of land which Matthew intended then they would be their closest neighbors.

The smell of baking wafted through the air, as Eliza and Matthew clattered up the porch steps and into the kitchen. Louisa was there and had just removed a pie from the oven. Setting it down to cool and dusting off her apron, she looked up at them and smiled. She looked different that day, the sad look which had so often appeared on her face in the weeks gone by now replaced with her old familiar smile.

"I was just beginning to wonder where you two had got to," she said, taking out plates from the cupboard and beckoning them to sit down.

"You didn't have to go to all this trouble, *Mamm*," Matthew said, but his mother only laughed.

"I wanted to, it isn't every day we have a betrothal to celebrate now, is it?" she said, and Eliza glanced at Matthew in surprise.

"That's why I wanted you to come around," he said, and Louisa nodded.

"Eliza, I've been a cruel and heartless woman these

past few weeks. You must have thought me quite terrible," she began.

Eliza protested, "Not at all, it must have been a shock to you to find out about the proposal. Perhaps we should have told you sooner. I know it's tradition to wait, but..." she began, but Louisa shook her head.

"No, I hold my hands up and say again, I was wrong and it's only after a lot of prayer and talking with Sarah Beiler and the Bishop that I realize that. The Lord has put into my heart a new song, that's what the scriptures say, and I'm pleased to say it's a song of happiness. I'm glad you two are getting married. Why I remember when Matthew was a little boy..." she said, and Matthew groaned.

"*Mamm*, do you have to?" he said, and she laughed.

"It's my prerogative... I remember when he was just a little boy, he told me that he was going to marry you, Eliza. Well, I'm pleased he is. And you were right in what you said, you're not taking him away from me. You'll be just across the fields and I won't take *nee* for an answer when I invite you both to dinner," she said, cutting generous pieces from the pie and placing it before them both ceremoniously.

Eliza smiled, she was happy to hear Louisa's words and to know that the two of them could now be reconciled. It was an answer to her own prayers, too, and she felt blessed that *Gott* had heard her and responded.

"There's still a lot to plan, it's not like we're just going to get married tomorrow," Matthew said, but his *mamm* shook her head.

"Don't leave it too long, you never know what might happen. *Nee*, I'm glad and I'll pray for you both, especially you, Eliza. You've got your work cut out," she said and offered them both another slice of pie.

When dinner was finished, Eliza and Matthew stepped out onto the porch, sitting together on the swing chair and looking out over the cornfields. He put his arm around her, and she rested her head on his shoulder, thinking over Louisa's words and wondering if now things might really be different.

"Did she really mean it?" Eliza asked, and Matthew turned to look at her in surprise.

"What do you mean?" he asked, and Eliza sat up, sighing as she chose her next words.

"I mean... well, does your *mamm* really mean she's happy for us... or is she just pretending? She seemed almost... too happy about it," Eliza replied, immediately feeling guilty for thinking such a thought.

"Of course she did. Why would she say it if she didn't mean it?" he asked, and Eliza shrugged her shoulders.

"I don't know. I just don't want her to say things she doesn't mean just because it'll make us happy," she replied.

"Listen, you should have seen how many times she went off to Bishop Beiler's house to see him and Sarah. She's prayed about it, she's thought about it, and she knows that this is what will make the two of us happy. That's all she wants, I promise you," Matthew said, leaning forward and kissing Eliza on the forehead.

But there was still a doubt in Eliza's heart, the thought that perhaps Louisa was only pretending to be glad for them, and really, deep down, she was still hurting at the prospect of losing Matthew and all which that would mean.

"I just want her to realize that I'm not taking you away from her. I love you, I love her, too. I just want us to be a family," Eliza replied.

"And we will be. I'll soon have the house built and then we can start our new life together, just wait and see, we'll be the happiest couple in all of Faith's Creek. I've prayed about it, too, and I know that *Gott's* will is for us to be happy, I just know it," he said.

Eliza forced a smile. "I know, I just want it all to be perfect," she replied, resting her head on his shoulder and dreaming of her wedding day and all that was to come.

CHAPTER SIX

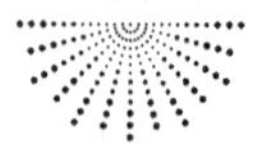

$\mathcal{A}$ few days later, and still, with doubts in her mind as to Louisa's true intentions, Eliza sat with her sisters on the porch. She was sewing, while Annie had her nose buried in a book and Patience was gazing out across the cornfields, as though lost in thought. It was a warm day, the heat of the summer seemed never-ending, and only the gentlest of breezes blew across the cornfields.

"I just can't cool down today, it's as though every ounce of energy has been sapped from me," Eliza said, fanning herself with her crochet frame and sighing.

"It'll break soon enough, it always does and you just wait until winter. When we're all huddled around the stove in the kitchen you'll dream about this day," Annie said, looking up from her book.

"What I wouldn't give for a blast of cold air right now, bring on the snow," Eliza said.

"We could go and get ice cream over at Bird-In-Hand, *Daed* might take us in the buggy," Patience said.

"I'm too hot to move, I think I'll just stay here and melt," Eliza replied.

"I'll get you some lemonade from inside, it won't be long before you're running after Matthew all day long, then you'll wish you were just sitting here with your sisters," Patience said, and she got up and went inside, calling to their *mamm* for a jug and some glasses.

"She's excited about the wedding, we all are," Annie said, turning to Eliza and smiling.

"It seems so long since Matthew asked me to marry him. I've never known a summer like this before. It seems to have stretched on in one endless hot, sunny day," Eliza replied, as Patience returned with a tray.

"There you are, freshly squeezed," she said, pouring

out a glass for Eliza, "you have the top, I know you prefer it sharp."

The sour taste of the lemonade caused Eliza to make a face and she laughed, as Patience stirred the jug around with a large spoon and poured a further two glasses, one for herself and one for Annie.

"I need a bit of sugar, Patience. I'm not that sweet already," she said.

"You must be pretty sweet, else Matthew wouldn't have asked you to marry him," Patience said, settling herself back down.

"I've just been lucky, that's all. You'll find someone, Patience, you're only young, you both will," Eliza replied, taking another sip of lemonade, and screwing up her face.

"We don't all want to get married," Annie said, and now it was Patience's turn to make a face.

"Of course, you do, why wouldn't you? You're just saying that because you've not found a man that wants to marry you yet," she replied, and Annie gave her a withering look.

"How do you know I haven't had offers? I might have

had a dozen proposals and turned them all down," she said.

Patience laughed. "Name them? I bet you haven't had any," she said, and Eliza put her glass down and raised her hands.

"Enough bickering. Patience, it's not everyone's dream to get married, you know. Annie wants to be a teacher and she can't be having a man following after her all the time if she's doing that now, can she?" Eliza said.

Patience shrugged. "I'd like it," she replied.

Eliza glanced at Annie, who shook her head and returned to her books. Of her two sisters, Annie was by far the more sensible one, while Patience was often lost in visions of romance, the likes of which only came true in storybooks. Still, she loved them both dearly, but they were like chalk and cheese, while Eliza seemed caught between the two, in age, looks, and attitude. She knew that romance came far harder than Patience believed, but unlike Annie, she had always believed she could have the life she wanted and find the man of her dreams.

"Then perhaps you'd better start looking, though I

think *Mamm* and *Daed* would be happier if you decided what you're going to do with your life and… oh," Annie said, pointing across the garden fence to where Eliza now saw their *daed* running at full pelt along the track leading to the house.

"What's wrong do you think?" Patience gasped, for their *daed* appeared to be in a terrible state, calling out to them to come quickly.

"What's happened *Daed*? Are you all right?" Eliza called out, hurrying down the steps of the porch her heart pounding with fear against her chest, as their *daed* pushed through the gate and up the path through the vegetable plot.

He looked as though he had seen a ghost, his face ashen, his hands trembling, and he clutched hold of Eliza, as Annie and Patience ran to her side.

"*Daed*, what's wrong? Is someone hurt?" Patience asked, and their *daed* nodded, his words garbled and confused.

"There's been an accident, over at the Lloyd place, I've just come from there. Come quickly, oh, it's terrible," he cried, as Eliza's heart skipped a beat.

"Matthew? Is it Matthew, *Daed*? Has something happened to him?" she cried, tears welling up in her eyes.

But their *daed* only shook his head, hurrying them along the track and making little sense in his explanations. The home of Matthew and his parents was only half a mile away, but it seemed the furthest that Eliza had ever run, so anxious was she to know what had happened. Outside, a small crowd had gathered and there was uproar and confusion. Doctor Yoder had just arrived and was making his way inside, a grave expression on his face. Bishop Beiler was there, too, he hurried to meet them, as Eliza burst into tears.

"Wait a moment, don't go running in there, just let Doctor Yoder do his work," the Bishop said, catching Eliza by the arm.

"What's happened? Is Matthew hurt? I need to go to him," she cried, but Amos kept a tight hold of her.

"It isn't Matthew, it's Louisa," he said, and Eliza looked at him in astonishment.

She had worked herself up into such a frenzy, imagining the very worst of everything, that it had not occurred to her to think of anyone else but Matthew. Now, she turned to Annie and Patience, who both wore grave looks on their faces, looking to her *daed*, who had removed his hat and bowed his head.

"Is she...?" Eliza whispered, and Amos sighed.

"Let Doctor Yoder see to her now. The best thing we can do is pray," he said, holding out his hands.

They formed a circle, Eliza, Bishop Amos Beiler, Annie, Patience, and their *daed*. Together, they prayed in silence and Eliza thanked *Gott* for delivering Matthew safely from harm. But in her prayer, she could not help but feel guilt at the thought of neglecting Louisa from her concerns and she tried her best to pray that she be delivered from this terrible tragedy, whatever it might be.

As they finished praying, the door to the house opened and Eliza looked up to see Matthew emerging with his *daed* and Doctor Yoder. She wanted to run to his side and embrace him, to tell him that everything would be all right and that she loved him. But something held her back and Bishop Beiler hurried over, exchanging several words with

Matthew's *daed*, he patted him reassuringly on the shoulder.

"Should I go to him, *Daed*?" she asked, and her father took hold of her hand.

"Wait a moment, Eliza," he said, and she watched, as Matthew turned away and put his head in his hands, walking off across the porch and standing with his head bowed, as though taken up by some awful sorrow.

"I have to go to him," Eliza said, pulling away from her *daed* and hurrying to Matthew's side.

"Eliza, wait," Annie called after her, but Eliza was gone.

"Matthew, what's happened? Oh, I was so worried when *Daed* came running. Is Louisa all right? She'll be all right, won't she? Doctor Yoder is a wonderful physician, he saw us all through the pox, and..." Eliza began, but she stopped herself short when she realized that Matthew was in tears.

She had never seen him cry before, not like this. There had been grazed knees and twisted ankles when they were children, tears of pain soon consoled, but this was different. His whole body was heaving with great shuddering sobs, tears running down his cheeks. She put out her hand to touch him, wanting only to comfort him in his grief.

"She fell... she fell down the stairs and she hasn't opened her eyes yet. She hasn't spoken, she hasn't moved. She's just lying there on the bed with her face all bruised up," he gasped, as Eliza put her arms around him.

"Oh, Matthew... there, there, oh, goodness I... it'll be all right, *Gott* won't take her away," she said, trying to make her words sound reassuring, though she knew in her heart how hollow and empty they must sound.

"Doctor Yoder says all we can do now is pray. She... she might never wake up. I saw it happen, I saw her trip from the top step. I don't know what she fell on, but she just tumbled, and... oh..." he wailed, fresh sobs now rising through him, Eliza's shoulder becoming damp from his tears.

"We mustn't worry until we know what's happened," Eliza said, as much trying to convince herself as him, "your *mamm* is strong, she's determined, it'll be all right, you'll see."

But just then, Matthew's *daed* approached and the two of them looked up, Eliza watching as Isaac shook his head.

"Matthew, will you come inside, please. I'm sorry..." he began, but he could not finish his words, tears rolling down his cheeks, as Matthew let out a fresh wail and clutched at Eliza.

"I'm so sorry," she whispered.

But there were no words which could console him, for the tragedy was almost too great to comprehend. At length, Matthew and his *daed* returned inside, along with Bishop Beiler and Doctor Yoder. Louisa had died of her injuries and there was nothing more that any earthly medicine could do for her.

"Come along, Eliza, we'll go home now," her *daed* said, taking Eliza by the arm, as she stood looking forlornly at the closed door, through which Matthew had made his way a few moments earlier to see his *mamm* in this world for the last time.

"I should stay... I should do something," Eliza said, but her *daed* shook his head.

"You've had as much of a shock over all of this as we

all have. You've not experienced death like this before. It takes time to come to terms with. It's the shock that's the worst thing and we're all in shock, the whole district is. The best thing you can do now is come along home and get some rest," he replied, taking her by the arm and leading her to where Annie and Patience were waiting by the gate.

In silence, the four of them walked home, where they found their own *mamm* in tears, for Sarah Beiler had just called by with the news. She looked up at them and shook her head, sobbing into a handkerchief, as Eliza went to comfort her.

"Oh, it's too awful, it's not fair, oh, why?" Barbara cried as Eliza put her arms around her.

"I don't know, *Mamm*, I don't know," she said. The two of them held one another, the whole family sitting dejected and sorrowful.

All anyone could think about in the days to come was Louisa and the tragedy of a life cut short by a mere accident, an accident that should never have happened. Eliza wanted to be a comfort to Matthew, to tell him that everything would be all right, but he seemed distant, avoiding her and shutting in on himself so that she was at a loss as to what to do.

"You've got to give him time, Eliza," her *mamm* told her, but the more time that passed, the more despairing Eliza felt of ever being able to help Matthew and regain the happiness they had been so close to achieving.

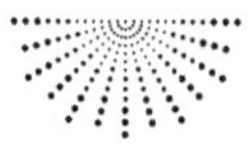

The days following the funeral were the hardest of Matthew's life. He felt numb, devoid of feeling, and angry, too. He had shed all the tears he possessed, or so it seemed, and now it seemed like life stretched out, empty and meaningless before him. He found himself questioning *Gott*, questioning why his *mamm* had been so cruelly taken from them and in such a tragic and heartbreaking way. He could make no sense of it and took to shutting himself away, unwilling to speak with anyone.

When Eliza called, he told his *daed* to send her away, for he had no wish for her to see him in such a way, spiraling into the depths of despair. The sight of his *mamm* falling down the stairs remained with him, haunting his waking thoughts, and he began to question whether there was something he could have done to prevent the accident from occurring. If only he had been there at the top of the stairs or spoken to her before she fell.

But such thoughts only served to increase his sense of self-loathing, a feeling which grew into a realization that if he could not protect his own *mamm*, then surely, he could not protect Eliza either. He began to have doubts about their marriage, not about his feelings for her, but about whether he could truly be the husband she deserved. There was a sense of inadequacy building within him, a feeling that he would never live up to the ideals he believed he should aspire to.

"I know it's hard, Matthew, I'm feeling it, too," his *daed* said, three days after the funeral, when the two of them had sat over dinner in silence, neither touching the hotpot which Sarah Beiler had brought them earlier that afternoon.

"I can't eat, I can't sleep, I just feel numb, worse than that, I don't feel anything," Matthew said, pushing his plate away and slumping back in his chair.

"Your *mamm* wouldn't have wanted this. She wouldn't have wanted to see either of us like this," his *daed* replied, shaking his head.

"Then why did she have to go leave us then?" Matthew cried, bringing his fist down hard on the table.

"It's all right, Matthew, I know you're hurting."

Matthew leaped to his feet, as tears welled up in his eyes.

"You don't know, *Daed*, you don't ..." he began, but just then, there came a gentle tap at the door and the voice of Bishop Beiler calling out to them.

"Isaac, Matthew? I just stopped by to see if you're all right," he said.

Matthew took a deep breath. It seemed that everyone was intent on making sure he was all right, even if it was clear that he was not. He went to answer the door, as his *daed* hastily hid the uneaten hot pot, and found Amos standing on the porch in the cool evening air.

"Thanks for coming, Bishop Beiler," Matthew said,

holding out his hand to the Bishop, who smiled and shook it.

"My pleasure, Matthew. Say, it's a nice evening, why don't the two of us take a walk? I'd like to see the plot of land you're planning to build on," he said.

Matthew nodded. He had barely left the house since the day of the funeral and he knew that the fresh air would do him good. He called out a goodbye to his *daed* and followed the bishop across the garden and out onto the track in front of the house. He was still not in the mood to talk, but in Amos's company, he felt at ease. The two of them walked side by side in silence for a while, the birds singing their evening chorus all around.

"Do you think animals grieve, Amos?" Matthew asked.

"In their own way they do, I'm sure. Swans mate for life, and why would the birds of the air have such beautiful songs if they didn't know both sorrow and joy? I'm pretty certain they grieve in their own way, just as you're doing, too," he said.

"I just can't see a way past it," Matthew admitted.

It was the first time he had voiced his feelings. He had barely been able to speak to Eliza, as much as he knew it upset her to realize that. His *daed* had his own way of dealing with grief and had spent hours in the barn chopping wood, anything to distract himself from the truth they now had to face.

"Did anyone say you had to? Grief isn't a set timetable, you know. It doesn't follow a pattern of days, as much as our forebears might have thought it did. We don't just wish our loved ones farewell and then get on with our lives. Their memory stays with us. Your *mamm* was taken from you, Matthew, taken in a cruel way and I don't have answers as to why that was. I wish I did, with all my heart," Amos said.

Matthew swallowed and fought back his tears. "I'm angry, I'm angry with *Gott*. I can't just move on, I can't forget this. Why did *Gott* take my *mamm* away?" he cried, clenching his fists.

They had arrived at the plot of land along the track, a place which only a few days before had seemed so filled with hope. Now, it represented everything that Matthew wanted to forget, the future he had planned with Eliza, a future that was shattered by this overwhelming tragedy.

"That's understandable, Matthew. No one can expect you not to be. We're all angry, we're all hurting."

Matthew shook his head. "Not like I am, it's me that's lost his *mamm*. I won't ever see her again, do you know how hard that is?" he cried, turning to the Bishop, who put his arm gently on Matthew's shoulder.

"I know what it's like to lose someone you love, Matthew, I know that. But you're dwelling on the tragedy instead of thinking about the life your *mamm* lived and the way she lived it. Your *mamm* was a good soul, a *Gott* loving soul, and she's found her salvation in heaven. You will see her again. Isn't that something to cling to? To hold onto and rejoice in?" he said.

Try as he might, Matthew could not bring himself to accept it. He had always accepted his faith and felt sorry for those who did not believe. But now, it seemed as though his faith had been tested and found wanting. He could not understand why *Gott* would take away the most precious thing in all the world, the love of his mother, and replace it with this hollow emptiness he now felt, an emptiness he thought could never be filled again.

"You know, I guess you remember what I was like as a child?" Matthew said, sitting down on a patch of dry grass by the gate into the meadow.

"You were a strange boy, and I don't mean that disrespectfully, but you had a certain way about you. You were awkward around just about everyone... though you turned out all right in the end," Amos said, sitting down next to Matthew and picking a stray sheaf of corn, which he proceeded to chew.

"It was only my *mamm* that believed in me... well, and Eliza, too. They each thought I was something special. If it weren't for them... I don't know what I'd be now."

"I'm sure you'd have turned out all right," Amos replied, but Matthew shook his head.

"No, you don't understand. It's not just that. I always felt I owed my *mamm* so much for what she did for me, I owed it to her to take care of her and be there for her. But I couldn't do it, could I? I was right there and I couldn't save her. And if I couldn't save her, then how can I look Eliza in the eyes and make my vows? How can I tell her I'll take care of her when I couldn't even take care of my own *mamm*?" he said, shaking his head and sighing.

Amos paused for a moment, the birds singing in the trees above and the gentle meandering of the creek below the only sounds that filled the air.

"You can't blame yourself," he said at last, "Doctor Yoder said there was nothing anyone could have done. It was an accident, Matthew. A terrible accident, but an accident, nonetheless. You couldn't have saved her and imagining that you could have done is only going to make things worse. You can spend your whole life living like this or accept that sometimes tragic things occur and we're not meant to fathom *Gott's* purposes."

"I should have done more," Matthew said, rising to his feet, he dusted himself off and wished Bishop Beiler a good evening.

He wasn't ready to go home yet and made his way along the path by the creek, watching the water lap over the rocks. There was a deep pool there, one in which he used to swim as a child, despite his *mamm* warning him of the dangers. He paused there, taking up a stone and throwing it into the waters, where it gave off a ripple, emanating out into nothingness.

Matthew knew that Bishop Beiler was only trying to help, as was his *daed*, but this was his grief, and he would deal with it in his own way. Despite everything, he could not rid himself of that terrible thought that he had been unable to save his *mamm* and that one day he might be unable to save Eliza from whatever cruel fate life might throw at them. He felt angry, his fists clenched and tears welled up in his eyes.

He was unsure how much longer he sat by the creek, though the sun had not yet set when he emerged from the trees and took the track toward Eliza's house. Despite everything, he still felt guilty for ignoring her, knowing that she too had only wanted to help. As he came in sight of the porch, he could see Annie sitting on the swing chair and reading. He had always liked Annie, her sharp wit and intellect were as formidable as that of his own *mamm*. When she saw him, she set down her book and hurried down to meet him, holding out her arms to embrace him as she did so.

"We've been hoping you'd come, Eliza especially. She misses you," Annie said.

Matthew swallowed his tear. "I was a fool to stay away, but... can I talk to her. I've got a lot on my mind," he replied.

Annie smiled and hurried into the house, calling out for her sister.

The sun was setting over the cornfields now, a slight chill in the air, Matthew leaned against the fence, not wanting to go inside. He knew that Eliza's family would make a fuss of him if he did and he didn't want to cause a scene, hoping to just speak with Eliza and say what he had to say. A moment later, she appeared on the porch and Annie bid him goodnight, before returning inside. He looked up at her shyly and she came to take him by the hand, the two of them walking along the track for a short distance until they were out of hearing from the house.

"I wasn't sure if you'd want to see me yet," she said.

"It wasn't that, I just needed some time. I've felt so numb these past few days. It's like everyone else is moving on, but I can't," he said, fighting back the tears in his eyes.

"You don't have to, you don't have to do anything you don't want to. You're grieving for your *mamm*, I understand that," she said, squeezing his hand.

"I've been thinking, Eliza. In fact, I've done nothing but think these past few days. I just spoke with Bishop Beiler, too. There's something about this place now, about Faith's Creek. Everywhere I look, I'm reminded of her and what's worse, I think if it weren't for this place, she might still be alive," he said.

Eliza looked up at him in astonishment. "What do you mean? You're not making sense, Matthew."

Only to Matthew, it made perfect sense. "The way we live, everything about it, that's why she died. If we'd been nearer a hospital, nearer other doctors, or something..." he began, the tears now rolling down his cheeks.

"It was an accident, Matthew. It wouldn't have mattered if we lived in New York City, Los Angles, San Francisco, or anywhere else. She fell down the stairs and that's that, there was nothing you could have done to save her." Eliza looked up at him with wide eyes, a tear rolling down her cheek.

"I'm sorry, Eliza. I can't do it, I can't stay here any longer, not feeling like this," he replied.

He knew that Eliza would be astonished by his words, that the very idea of leaving Faith's Creek was alien to her, and that he was forcing her to choose between her family and him. But try as he might, and despite the irrationality of it all, he could not help but blame himself for his *mamm's* death. He was terrified that he would fail to protect Eliza, too, and the only way he knew of safeguarding her was for them to leave. To leave Faith's Creek behind and return to the world which each of them had experienced during the turbulent times of their Rumspringa.

Eliza was silent for a moment and he wondered what she was thinking. Was she even now having doubts about their marriage? Perhaps she was thinking how simpler life would be without him, a thought which caused his heart to skip a beat. He was so in love with her, so much so that the thought of losing her was like a dagger to his heart. But neither could he bear to remain in a place which had brought such unhappiness on him and caused him to question everything he had once held dear.

"I can understand that you're upset, Matthew. Truly I can, but running away isn't the answer," she said, shaking her head.

"I'm not running away, I just don't want to be here anymore, I can't be here anymore," he whispered, suddenly feeling an overwhelming exhaustion come over him.

It was as though all his energy was spent, every emotion used up, and now he felt only numbness and pain. He wanted to sleep forever, to forget everything and drift away, to go back to feeling as he had done only days before, when everything had seemed so bright and the future had laid open ahead of them, filled with possibility.

"But we can't just leave Faith's Creek. This is our home, it's where our roots are. I don't want to leave my family, I can't leave them. Surely you understand that?" she said.

Matthew fought back the tears. "You mean you can stay here? Even after everything that's happened?

Where's *Gott* in all of this? Not here, that's for certain," Matthew said.

Eliza gasped and her hand flew to her chest. "Matthew, *Gott* didn't take your *mamm* away from you. You're loved, she's found her salvation in heaven..." Eliza began, but Matthew did not want to hear it.

He was tired of hearing excuses for why his *mamm* had been taken from him. There could be no reason for it, no logic, no rationality. As far as Matthew was concerned, *Gott* had taken his *mamm* from him and there could be no reasonable explanation for that, no comfort, only sorrow.

"*Gott* isn't watching over Faith's Creek, not if this can happen, and I can't stay here a moment longer, not with knowing that," he said, though part of him knew this was illogical, he couldn't stop the feelings. The betrayal, the loss, it was too much, he pulled away from her.

"Matthew, what are you saying?" she asked.

Matthew could not bear to remain at her side a moment longer. With one last, imploring look, he turned his back on her, striding off along the path through the vegetable patch, as she called out after him.

"I can't do it, Eliza, I'm too full of doubts," he called back, as tears rolled down his cheeks.

"Isn't my love enough to keep you here?" she called out after him.

Matthew swallowed down the words that wanted to shout *jah*, he could not bear to answer. With the heaviest of hearts, he fled, leaving behind the woman he loved too much to risk losing as he had done his *mamm*...

CHAPTER EIGHT

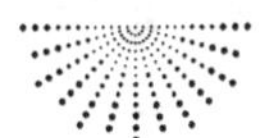

"**W**on't you eat something, Eliza?" her *mamm* asked, holding a pan of eggs in her hand.

Eliza shook her head. "I don't feel like eating anything, sorry *Mamm*," she said.

"Some coffee then, you need something inside you. You can't just exist on thin air," she said, as Annie and Patience came clattering down the stairs.

"Still nothing?" Annie asked as she sat down at the table and their *mamm* placed two eggs on her plate.

"It's been three days now since I heard from him. I

don't know what to do. I can't sleep, I can't eat, I can't concentrate on anything," Eliza said.

"I'm sure he'll come around in the end. You've got to give him time, he's got so much to deal with at the moment. You read about it in books, the way people grieve is all different," Annie began.

"This isn't a book," Eliza snapped at her. "This is a real person and real people don't always behave like your books tell you," she cried, a well of emotion erupting inside her, as tears rolled down her cheeks.

"Oh, Eliza, I was just trying to make it better for you," Annie said, and their *mamm* sighed.

"Look, Eliza, how would it be if your *daed* took you over to the Lloyd place this morning? You don't have to go on your own and perhaps you and Matthew can talk. I hate to see you like this, we all do," she said.

Eliza shrugged her shoulders and then smiled at her sister. "I'm sorry, Annie, I didn't mean to shout at you. It's just... oh, I can't leave Faith's Creek to go with him, but I don't want him to leave either," she said, voicing the impossibility of her situation.

"Which is why you need to talk to him and resolve

this matter, isn't that right Samuel?" their *mamm* said, just as their *daed* entered the kitchen for his breakfast.

He was carrying a basket of vegetables and looked confused, as Barbara held up the pan of eggs.

"Talk to who?" Samuel asked, and Barbara sighed and rolled her eyes. "Men, their heads are often in the clouds." She smiled at him. "To Matthew. I told Eliza that you'd take her over to the Lloyd place this morning so that the two of them can talk. This has gone on long enough, we can't have them not speaking to one another. Look how upset Eliza is."

"Let me eat my breakfast first and then we'll go," he said, as Barbara served him two eggs and offered him a cup of coffee.

Around half an hour later, Eliza found herself in the buggy with her *daed*. It was a fresh, clear morning, with a mist hanging over the cornfields and a slight chill in the air, a reminder that autumn was fast approaching. Eliza was wearing her normal work dress and shawl, her kapp on her head, and a freshly baked apple pie in her basket. It was a peace offering for Matthew in the hope that they might talk.

"Your *Mamm* was pretty insistent that you talk to him," Samuel said, and Eliza sighed.

"She's right, we need to talk. I just hope he'll listen to sense."

"I thought about it once, leaving, I mean," Samuel said and Eliza's eyes widened in surprise. "But... it just wasn't the right thing, not in the end... not for me. The world out there... well, it's different to what you think."

"You don't need to tell me that," Eliza said, as something caught in her throat and she began to cough.

"Frog got your voice?" Samuel asked as Eliza gasped for air.

The coughing grew worse and he pulled the horse up and slapped her back with the palm of his hand.

"Are you okay?" there was concern in his voice.

"I'll be all right, I keep getting this tickling cough," she replied, finally getting a breath.

"It's the change in the air, these cold mornings, then the heat during the day. That and the worry, you'll be fine," he said, as he clicked the horse into a trot and soon they pulled up outside the Graber house.

Eliza was nervous, she was unsure of what to say, though she had prayed to *Gott* for guidance and knew that the right words would come if she let them. As they pulled up, Isaac appeared from one of the sheds, he was carrying an ax, it seemed he had risen early to chop wood, his brow dripped sweat and his dungarees were covered in wood chippings.

"The early bird," Samuel said, and Isaac nodded.

"I don't sleep well at the moment, Samuel, you know how it is."

Samuel nodded ad offered him a smile of understanding. "We came because it's about time that Eliza and Matthew talked. They can't go on like this forever," he said and pointed toward the house.

"Jah," Isaac said coming to help her down from the buggy. "You'd better go in, Eliza. He's in a bad way. I appreciate you coming and just hope you can reach him."

"I'm sorry for your loss too," she said and let herself into the house, the familiarity of which seemed tainted by recent events. She had once felt so at home here, but now it seemed almost unwelcoming. From upstairs, she could hear the sound of Matthew muttering to himself and she hurried up to the landing, calling out to him as she went.

"Matthew, it's Eliza, can we talk?" she said.

A lump blocked her throat and her heart pounded against her chest as he appeared at his bedroom door, a pile of shirts in his arms. Was he packing? Was he about to leave, even without saying goodbye?

"I was going to tell you," he said, as color flooded his cheeks. Perhaps he could still read her mind?

"Are you leaving?" she gasped, following him into his bedroom, which was strewn with clothes, two open cases sat on a bed piled high with clothes.

"I told you, I don't have a choice," he replied, shaking his head sadly.

"Oh, Matthew, please don't leave. You know how much I love you, can't we work this out? I don't want you to leave," she gasped, clutching hold of his arm.

But he shook her off and turned away, tossing another pile of clothes into one of the cases.

"I can't stay here any longer. The memories are unbearable, the worry, the guilt... but I don't have to go alone, why don't you come with me? That's what I said from the start. I love you, Eliza, but I can't stay here. Come with me. We can start a new life somewhere else, far away from here. Somewhere we'll be safe," he said.

Eliza was astonished by his words. How could he possibly make her choose between him and her family? It wasn't just about Faith's Creek, this was about all she held dear, all that they both held dear. How could he throw it all away and leave?

"You can't mean it, Matthew. You can't really abandon your faith, everything you've always held dear?" she said, catching hold of his arm and forcing him to look at her.

"I can if it's abandoned me," he said, as tears welled up in his eyes.

"But this is everything you've ever known. It's all that either of us knows. The world's a different place, it's not like Faith's Creek. We can't just start over again. I can't leave my family and I can't abandon my faith," she said, her hands trembling, as she stared at him.

The world seemed to slow but it would never stop, not even for her and her love. It was like sand running through her fingers, for she knew that there could be no persuading him. There was a determination in his eyes, as though he had decided already what to do, with or without her.

"If that's your final choice, then there's nothing I can do to change your mind. But I'm telling you, Eliza. I can't stay here and if you're no longer going to have my back like you always have done... well, I suppose we don't have much else to say to one another," he said.

Eliza was too shocked to speak, filled with nothing but sorrow at his words. It seemed that the choice had been made for her and that Matthew would leave without her. There was nothing she could do, hot tears ran down her cheeks, as she sought desperately for words to fill the void she felt.

"But I... I love you," was all she could whisper.

"And I love you, too, but I can't love this place, not anymore and I can't stay here. I'm sorry," he said.

Her breathing was erratic, the shock of what he had said almost too much to bear and she began to cough, steadying herself against the wall she tried to catch her breath. She didn't need this, not now!

"I..." she began, but the coughing overtook her, and she spluttered into her handkerchief, as Matthew turned to her in alarm.

"Are you all right?" he asked.

Eliza shook her head, the cough had brought with it a touch of defiance and anger. How could he throw away their love? She didn't need his sympathy. "You don't need to worry about that anymore," she said, and without waiting for his reply, she fled, clattering down the stairs and out onto the porch.

Isaac and Samuel stood talking by the buggy, they looked up in surprise, as Eliza stumbled toward them. Her cough had grown worse now, and she rasped and heaved, steadying herself on the porch rail, as her *daed* hurried over.

"Eliza, are you all right?" Isaac asked, as Samuel hastily pulled up a chair for her to sit on.

"I'll be all right, could I have some water... I... oh..." she gasped, and before she could finish her words, Eliza fainted.

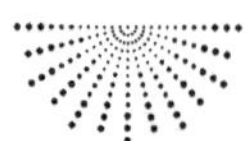

Matthew threw another half dozen shirts into one of the cases and slammed the lid shut with a bang. He was angry with Eliza, angry that she would not stay loyal to him, and angry that his feelings forced him to leave the place he loved. He could not bear the thought of remaining there a moment longer and yet in leaving, he was abandoning everything he had ever known. He listened as Eliza clattered down the stairs and then went to the window, his heart heavy at the thought of seeing her leave.

But he was surprised to see his father and Samuel by the buggy, the two of them now hurrying back toward the house and the sounds of a commotion erupted from below. He rushed from his bedroom and almost tripped at the top of the stairs, cursing to himself as he was reminded of the tragedy he was trying to escape. Had something happened to Eliza? All other thoughts but Eliza left him and he raced down the stairs, pulled open the front door, and hurried out onto the porch. Samuel was cradling Eliza in his arms.

"What happened?" he cried, kneeling at her side, and taking her by the hand.

"She was coughing and then she fainted, I don't know what's wrong with her. I need to get Doctor Yoder, will you take care of her for me?" Samuel asked, his eyes wide and worried.

"Don't you worry about that," Isaac said. "We'll get her inside and make her comfortable, won't we, Matthew? Come on, help me now."

Samuel hurried off to the buggy, geeing up the horse and racing off along the track toward the town.

"Eliza, are you all right? Oh, please wake up," Matthew cried, clutching hold of Eliza's hand.

All thoughts of leaving were pushed aside and his heart was beating fast at seeing Eliza unconscious. He felt helpless, just as he had done on the day of his *mamm's* death. For a moment he wondered if he would lose her too. Was this his fate? To lose anyone he loved??

"Help me, Matthew, we need to lift her inside," Isaac said, and Matthew eased his arms beneath Eliza, the two of them carrying her into the house and laying her on the sofa in the corner of the room.

"I can't do it, *Daed*, I can't lose her, not so soon after *Mamm*. Oh, Eliza, won't you wake up, oh, please, wake up," Matthew implored, kneeling at her side.

But Eliza did not open her eyes, appearing as though in a deep sleep, her head flopped to one side and her face pale and cold to the touch.

"Wait until Doctor Yoder gets here, he'll know what to do," Isaac said.

Matthew shook his head. "*Nee, nee, nee*, I can't lose her. She'll wake up and then I'll take her far, far away from here, somewhere safe, where we can both be together," he said, his words muddled and confused. It was too much. His heart was wracked with sorrow and grief, the thought of losing Eliza was too much to bear.

"Be careful what you're saying, Matthew. She doesn't want to leave Faith's Creek, her family is here, everything she loves is here, including you." Isaac paused and looked as if he was praying for a moment. "Your *mamm* wouldn't want either of you to leave, can't you see that. She wouldn't want you to run away, running away isn't the answer. She'd want you to stay and come to terms with what's happened. All of us want to run away at times, but it doesn't help. Problems follow you, life is life with all its glories and all its tragedies wherever you are. The past has a nasty way of catching up with you." Isaac placed his hand gently on Matthew's shoulder.

Matthew clutched at Eliza's hand, imploring her to wake up. He loved her so much and he wanted nothing but to see her safe and well. The sight of her lying on the porch had shocked him, filling him with dread at the thought of how easily she too could be snatched away from him. Life was precious and fragile, so easily taken away. Now, he knelt at her side, desperate to see signs of life in her, longing for her to open her eyes so that he could tell her he loved her. That he would always love her.

"She'll be all right, she'll be all right," he repeated, glancing out of the window, and urging help to come.

"Pray for her, Matthew, that's what we can do," Isaac said.

Matthew tried but last time his prayers had been ignored, he could not do it now. He could not pray, not when another life he held so dear hung in the balance.

After what seemed to be an age, the sounds of a buggy came from outside and footsteps soon clattered on the porch. Isaac hurried to open the door and a moment later, Doctor Yoder was at Matthew's side, opening his medical bag and listening to Eliza's heartbeat with his stethoscope.

The rest of Eliza's family had arrived too, her sisters looking anxiously on, as her *mamm* rushed to her daughter's side.

"Oh, Matthew, thank you for staying with her. What's wrong with her Doctor Yoder? She's going to be all right, isn't she?" Barbara asked.

The doctor stuck his thermometer into Eliza's mouth and thought for a moment. Then he nodded and his face relaxed into a smile. "It's a cold, it's settled on her lungs, but I promise you, I'll do everything I can to help her. Perhaps you might all step back a moment and let me work," he said.

"Come on, Matthew, let's give Doctor Yoder some space," Barbara said, giving Matthew a weak smile.

Matthew was reluctant to leave Eliza's side, even if only for a moment, but he rose to his feet, shaking his head and putting his hands together. He wanted to pray and find the faith to see him through this terrible ordeal, but try as he might, the words just would not come.

The family gathered in the kitchen, each with grave faces, as they waited for Doctor Yoder to give them fresh news of Eliza's condition. The clock on the wall ticked away and it felt like a hammer to Matthew's skull, tick, tick, tick, as he paced up and down.

"I can't bear this any longer," he cried.

His *daed* caught hold of him and shook his head. "Can't you see that everyone is suffering? We're all worried about Eliza."

Barbara nodded. "The best thing we can do right now is to pray. Won't you pray with us, Matthew?" she asked, as the family all joined hands.

But Matthew could not bring himself to pray, he stepped back, shaking his head and watching, as the Grabers closed their eyes and began to pray in silence. Matthew had said no prayers since before his *mamm's* death. He could not bring himself to speak to *Gott*, even in anger. As far as Matthew was concerned, *Gott* had abandoned them, and the events of that day were further proof of that.

It felt wrong to watch, to pretend as though he was part of something he could no longer bring himself to believe in. He stepped back into the parlor, where Doctor Yoder attended to Eliza. Once again, Matthew thought of leaving, of taking Eliza with him, for surely she could now be persuaded. He willed her to get better, so much so that it almost felt selfish, as though his own happiness would be determined by it, for how could he ever be happy again if Eliza was lost?

"Let me work, Matthew, don't stand there watching me," Doctor Yoder called out.

Matthew hurried out onto the porch, a feeling of nausea rising inside him. He wanted to be sick and his head ached, the strain of these past days overwhelmed him. Gasping for breath, he leaned on the porch rail, and looked out over the cornfields, just as the sounds of a buggy approaching could be heard along the track. It was Bishop Beiler and Sarah approaching, the two of them hurrying over to him with anxious looks on their faces.

"We came as soon as we heard, this is just awful," Amos said, shaking his head.

"Try not to worry, Matthew, I'm sure Doctor Yoder has everything under control," Sarah added, as Matthew fought back the tears in his eyes.

"I'll go in and speak to Isaac," Amos said, stepping past Matthew and into the house.

Sarah remained out on the porch, she put her hand out to touch Matthew's arm, giving him a reassuring smile, as tears ran down his cheeks.

"I know you must be so worried, Matthew, but this is different," she said,.

Matthew shook his head. "Is it? I can't do anything about it, I feel so helpless." He clenched his fists and kicked out at the porch rail, which buckled under the force of his assault.

"It's understandable to be angry, you've lost your *mamm* and now you're worried you'll lose Eliza, too. But none of this is your fault," Sarah said.

"No, it's *Gott*, where's *Gott* in all of this?" Matthew demanded.

Sarah smiled. "He's right here, suffering alongside us. *Gott's* love is here, in the people and in this place, surrounding us and bringing us hope. If you're finding that hard to believe at the moment then let us believe it for you, let us be that hope," she said.

Her words were not what he expected. "I... I don't understand," he whispered.

She reached out and squeezed his hand. "*Gott* didn't take away your *mamm,* Matthew. She had an accident, but I know one thing *Gott* did do. He gave you a loving *mamm,* a *mamm* who loved you more than anything else in the world. She wouldn't have wanted to see you like this, angry and blaming her death on yourself. I remember speaking to her after your engagement was announced, she was so worried about losing you, she hated the idea, but she wanted you to be happy, too," Sarah said.

"What... what did she say?" Matthew asked, brushing away his tears.

"She realized in the end that *Gott's* will was for you to be happy, to be married and that there was no one better than Eliza to make that happen. She loved you enough to let you go and that's what you have to do, too. She wouldn't want you to be held back by grief, just like she didn't want you to be held back by her feelings, either," Sarah replied.

"Or maybe she was just telling us what we wanted to hear," he replied, knowing how spiteful his words must sound.

"Now come on, Matthew. You know you don't believe that. When your *mamm* told you she was happy for you, she meant it, every word of it," Sarah said, fixing him with a resolute expression that caused him to falter.

"And now? What about Eliza?" Mathew asked.

Sarah smiled. "There's only one thing you need to do right now, and that's be there for her. Running away isn't the answer. Let us hold you in prayer and try it yourself, you might be surprised," she said, and with that, she made her way inside, leaving Mathew alone on the porch with his thoughts.

He sighed, leaning on the rail, and put his head in his hands. He thought about what Sarah had said, knowing that despite everything, he had still been held in prayer by those around him. Eliza had told him that and so had his *daed*. When he had found it impossible to pray, others had prayed for him. Now, Matthew looked up, longing to hear *Gott's* voice, longing to feel His presence as once he had done. He began to pray, imploring Eliza's safety and begging for her to wake up.

If only Eliza would be all right, then Matthew would

reclaim his faith. It felt like bargaining, but that was all he could find in himself to think. Urging *Gott* to hear his prayer, it became the pleading of a desperate man. He sank to his knees, his hands clasped together, his head bowed. He had never prayed so hard before, even if his heart was filled with doubts as to his own belief. His faith was shaken, but still, a light remained, the merest glimmer of hope that his prayers would be heard.

At last, he let his hands fall to his side, exhausted by the exertions of his prayer. His head was spinning, throbbing with the intensity of his thoughts. The energy had seemed to drain from him, as though this final act of desperation was his only hope. He pulled himself to his feet, as tears ran down his face. But there was nothing. No feeling in his heart, no words across his mind, only that same numbness and emptiness he had felt before. Was he to be denied? Bringing his fist down on the porch rail he kicked out in frustration. Where was *Gott* in all of this? Where was the answer to his prayer?

"Matthew, come quickly, come inside," a frantic voice behind him called out, and he turned to find Patience's anxious face at the door.

"What's happened? Is she all right?" Matthew cried.

Patience beckoned him. "Come and see, quickly now, come and see," she called out.

Matthew wasted no time in hurrying after her, his mind filled with dread at what he might find.

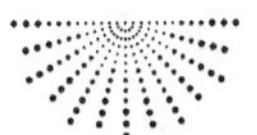

CHAPTER TEN

As he hurried inside, Matthew could hear voices coming from the parlor, he burst through the door, as Doctor Yoder stood up and nodded.

"Is she all right?" Matthew cried.

Doctor Yoder smiled. "She will be, I've given her some medication, as well as a ginger tea. It's a nasty fever, but nothing that a strong young lady like her won't make it through," he said, as Matthew rushed to Eliza's side.

Her eyes were open now and, though she still looked pale, some of the color had returned to her cheeks.

She smiled weakly at him, as he took her hand and brought it to his lips.

"Oh, Eliza, I've been so worried," he said, fighting back the tears in his eyes.

"What's say we give these two a moment alone?" Amos said, and the others trooped out into the kitchen, followed by Doctor Yoder, who assured them he would call again the next day.

"I thought I'd lost you, I thought you'd gone," he whispered, shaking his head, as though he could hardly believe the sight before his eyes.

Eliza only smiled and feebly squeezed his hand.

"I wasn't going to go that quickly," she whispered, beginning to laugh, and coughing as she did so.

"Be careful, try and rest, I'm right here," he said, reaching out to gently touch her face.

It still felt cold. He rubbed her fingers, desperate to bring some warmth to her.

"I thought you were going," she said.

He grimaced, knowing how close those words had

come to being true. "I'm sorry, I was a fool, I'm not leaving you, not ever. I promise you that, Eliza. I only want to be with you, to be where you want to be, that's all that matters," he said, surprised at the force of his own feelings.

He no longer wanted to leave Faith's Creek behind. Sarah had been right, as had his *daed*, the past would always catch up with him. It had not been Faith's Creek he had wanted to run away from, but the feelings inside him. Now, having come so close to losing Eliza, he realized how important it was to cling to what mattered, even if it meant some heartache along the way.

"Do you mean that?" she whispered, her eyes closing again.

He took her by both hands, willing her to get better. "With all my heart, I do. I won't ever leave you. I can't live without you and I was a fool to think I could. Don't you remember that time when we were children? The day I got pushed into the mud by those older boys. You came right along and picked me up, you even chased them away. Well, you've always been there to pick me up, dust me off and tell me everything's going to be all right. But that's my job, too. I need to be there for you and I will be," he said, as the faintest of smiles came over her face.

"I do remember," she said, opening her eyes and looking up at him, "they never bothered you again after that."

"No one would dare after they had you chasing after them through the town," Matthew replied, laughing, as he helped her to sit up.

Eliza's face was still pale, but her hands felt warmer now, he handed her the cup of ginger tea, which she sipped, before turning to look out of the window across the cornfields toward the creek and the meadows.

"Will you really stay?" she asked

"I promise you, I will, with all my heart. Can you forgive me for even thinking about leaving?" he asked.

"I can, but I don't ever want to think of losing you again," she said.

He shook his head and pointed at the window. "Do

you see out there, across the cornfields? That's where our house is going to be, that's where we'll be happy, right here in Faith's Creek where we belong," he said, and with those words, Matthew knew that all would be well.

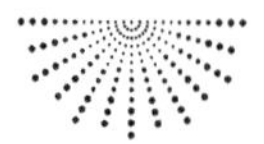

*E*liza made a good recovery, though it took some time to get over the fever. Doctor Yoder was diligent in his ministrations, prescribing a strict routine of rest and medication. They took her home, where she recuperated. Matthew was an almost constant presence and gradually his faith returned. The grief had taken its toll. He had been tested but as the days passed his faith grew stronger.

He knew it would be tested again but he also knew that next time he would understand. Gott did not wish to hurt him and He would be there beside him if He was needed. All Matthew had to do was learn to ask. It had been such a temptation to run from his troubles. To hope that space would take away the pain but he knew now that wouldn't have helped. If he had left, his pain would have gone with him but the support and love of his family would have been left behind. Now, he realized what a lonely life that would have been.

Each day of her recovery he brought her flowers or little gifts: a carved spoon, a book of poems, things for her Hope Chest. As she recovered he was ever diligent in his care for her. The months passed by, winter came and Eliza regained her strength, her one desire was to marry Matthew and live the happy life they had always dreamed of.

It was the day of their wedding and the whole community turned out to celebrate, the ceremony held in Mr. Jackson's barn and officiated over by Bishop Amos Beiler. There was much rejoicing, and even Betty Lapp turned out to wish the couple well. Annie and Patience acted as newehockers. Eliza was dressed in a plain blue dress, much like her everyday dress and yet somehow this one was special. Mathew had picked a posy of flowers for her to hold.

As she and Matthew emerged from the barn, arm in arm, a great shout of celebration went up from the congregation, all of whom had gathered to pray for them and wish them well.

Over the next few minutes, the barn would be transformed for the meal to follow. People bustled to and fro, congratulating the couple on the clear, bright, and sunny winter's day. Soon the food that Barbara and the other women had prepared was laid out on long trestle tables and the whole district surged back into the barn.

"What a beautiful day this is," Eliza said, resting her head on Mathew's shoulder, as the two of them sat at the back corner, surrounded by their family and friends.

"It'll be Annie next," Samuel said.

Barbara laughed. "I don't think so. Patience looks like she's already made her plans," she replied, pointing over to where Patience was talking to a handsome young man by the name of Levi Smucker.

"Are you going to say a few words, Matthew?" Samuel asked, and Matthew nodded.

"In a moment," he said, slipping his hand into Eliza's and beckoning him to follow her.

They left the guests enjoying the food and made their way across the farmyard to that same gate where Matthew had proposed to her back in May the previous year. A lot had changed since then, but one thing remained for certain and that was the love which each of them felt for the other. It was a love that was growing stronger by the day and which now they had affirmed before *Gott* and the district.

"Is everything all right?" Eliza asked.

Matthew smiled. "Is it wrong to want a moment alone with my *fraa?*" he asked.

Eliza blushed. "Not at all, I wanted to be alone with you, too," she replied.

"I can't believe we made it, finally we made it, after everything that's happened," he said, putting his arm around her, as the two of them leaned on the gate and gazed out over the cornfields.

She rested her head on his shoulder, caught up in the perfect moment they shared. She loved him so much and the thought of even coming close to losing him brought sorrow to her heart.

"We came close to losing it," she said.

He shook his head and sighed. "I know, and I'm sorry I tried to make you leave, to make you choose. That wasn't fair at all."

"I should have done more to help you," she admitted, but he shook his head.

"It's all in the past now, let's not have any more regrets. I wish my *mamm* was here to see this happy day, but I know she'd be happy for us. She loved you like you were her own and I know she wanted us to marry. I feel terrible for doubting my faith, she never doubted hers, not for one moment," he said.

Eliza slipped her hand into his. "Didn't you say '*nee* regrets'? You found that faith again and maybe you had to question it to make it stronger. We all question, I know I do, and I know why you did. The important thing is what happens now, how we live out our faith together," she said, smiling at him.

It was all she wanted, to be his *fraa* and for the two of them to make good the vows they had made that day. To love one another and do all they could to play their part as man and *fraa* in the community of Faith's Creek.

"I don't ever want another doubt, I just hope my

faith can be as strong as my *mamm's*, that would be a fitting legacy to her and the best way to remember her," he said, smiling at Eliza.

"She will be looking down on us and smiling. I know it. Now, all we can do is look ahead and have faith, that's where the adventure lies," Eliza said, and reaching up to him, she kissed him, knowing that it was faith, hope, and love that had brought them together and that that same trinity would sustain them for the rest of their lives.

The End.

Reade on for a Preview of the next book...

To be the youngest of three sisters is always hard. You are always watching your older sisters grow and spread their wings. You see them find their place in the world, while you are still looking for yours. You see them happy when your own dreams go unfulfilled. Such was the lot for Patience Graber who, at nineteen years old, had watched her eldest sister Annie realize her ambition to become a schoolteacher and her middle sister Eliza marry the man she loved. Now it was Patience who had to live up to her name. She was a romantic and dreamed of love. Her dreams of finding a husband were still unfulfilled and though she knew it was wrong to wish the time would come... she couldn't help herself.

"You're still young, Patience, you only had your rumspringa a season ago. Give it time, have patience, Patience," her mamm, Barbara Graber would reply when Patience made her feelings known.

But still, the thought remained, and as time went by, she longed to find a husband and settle down. In that regard, she took after her sister Eliza, and though she knew that jealousy was a terrible sin, she could not help but feel it in her heart whenever her sister and her handsome husband, Matthew, came to visit.

They lived in a farmhouse not far away across the cornfields, and Patience would often go and visit them, helping her sister with the animals or sharing a simple meal with them. But it always pained her to see how happy Eliza was in her new life. Though she was happy for her sister, she yearned of sharing that happiness by finding a romance of her own. Faith's Creek had been her home all her life. She loved its rolling landscape, pretty houses, and simple way of life; yet, she could not help but wonder if she would ever find a husband there.

The men of Faith's Creek were good men and though she had known many of them all her life, there was not one among them that attracted her. It was as though over-familiarity and the bonds of friendship prevented any romantic feelings from emerging, a fact which made Patience ever more impatient with her search.

"What about James Kauffman? He's a nice boy, he always says 'hello' when I pass by the farm if he's working in the fields. Perhaps I could introduce the two of you?" Barbara said one afternoon.

Patience bit back a sigh, she knew her *mamm* was trying to help and shook her head. "He's nice, but I've known him since I was knee-high. I want to meet someone new, someone I don't know yet," she replied, sighing, as she sat at the table. Her *mamm* was elbows deep in flour, for it was the morning of baking day, the kitchen already smelled of cinnamon and cloves, sweet and fragrant.

"Didn't you have enough of meeting new men during your rumspringa?" Barbara asked.

Patience smiled. "I don't want a man from just anywhere *Mamm*, he has to share our values, like Matthew does. Eliza's so happy, I just want that, too," she replied, as her eldest sister Annie came clattering down the stairs.

"Don't forget those work books there, Annie," Barbara said, pointing to a pile of books on the table.

"Oh, thank you, *Mamm*, I'd forget my head if it weren't screwed on. What a rush," she said, snatching up the books and kissing their *mamm* goodbye.

"Will you be back for dinner at noon?" Barbara called out, but Annie was gone, the porch door banging behind her.

"Now there's a girl who doesn't have time for a husband," Barbara said, and Patience smiled.

"I know not everyone wants to get married, but I do. Annie made up her mind a long time ago to be a schoolteacher, it's all she's ever wanted to do. But all I've ever wanted is to find a husband, and I can't even do that," she said, sighing and putting her head into her hands.

"Oh, Patience, enough of this. Sometimes, when I've lost something, I search and search for it and can't find it. But when I stop looking, it turns up, just like that. Maybe you should look a little less hard and not expect so much," Barbara replied with a chuckle.

"Do you need any help this morning or can I walk over to Eliza's?" Patience asked, and her *mamm* laughed.

"You've got a face that would turn milk today, Patience, and I don't think it'll be any help in raising bread and cakes. Go over to see your sister, tell her I said she has to cheer you up. Go on now," she said.

Patience kissed her mother's smooth cheek and straightened her kapp before stepping out into the sunshine. It was late July, the cornfields swaying gently in the breeze, a patchwork of golden colors spread out before her. The lane toward Faith's Creek wound its way across the fields, and she smiled at the sound of birds singing in the trees above.

"Off out already, Patience? Your sister was in such a rush she didn't even see me," her *daed*, Samuel called out.

He was weeding in the vegetable patch, his large straw hat all that was visible above the bean stalks growing up the trellis which ran the length of the patch.

"I'm going to see Eliza, *Mamm* said I could," Patience called out, and Samuel waved his hand.

"Say 'hello' to your sister from me, and tell Matthew I've got those seeds he wanted, though he'll have to be quick if he wants to plant them," he called back.

Patience set out to walk to the home of Eliza and Matthew. It was only a mile away, and as she walked, she greeted their friends and neighbors along the way. Her sister was outside feeding the chickens when Patience arrived, and she waved to her, beckoning her through the gate and hurrying to embrace her.

"This is a nice surprise, I thought you'd be helping *Mamm* with the baking," Eliza said.

She was a pretty woman, and Patience had always envied her looks. She considered herself to be somewhat plain, though in truth she was just as pretty as her sister, with blonde hair and blue eyes. Eliza's hair being darker; of course, you could hardly tell from the few strands that escaped her kapp.

"She said I was too miserable to help her bake, that nothing would rise if I stayed around," Patience replied, causing her sister to laugh.

"Well, don't bring that sour face in here, I don't want my milk turning. Come on in, I'll make us some coffee and you can tell me what's wrong. I'm sure it's not that bad." Eliza ushered Patience up the steps onto the porch.

Matthew had only just finished building the house and everything was brand new. It was a cozy place, the door opening into a parlor with a range and chairs, a sideboard and table, with a door leading into the kitchen beyond. Eliza had made cross-stitch pictures for the walls and woven a rug for the floor. Patience loved visiting her sister, even if in her company she was reminded of what she did not yet possess.

"Oh, *Daed* says that the seeds Matthew wants are ready, though you need to plant them quick," Patience said, settling herself down in her favorite chair by the stove.

"He's over at Bishop Beiler's house at the moment fixing the fence, we can tell him when he gets back. Now, what's the matter? I can see there's something not right," Eliza said, putting on a kettle to boil and coming to sit opposite Patience, who sighed.

"Why don't prayers get answered?" she asked.

Eliza looked at her in surprise. "What a thing to say,

Patience, you know they do, but you also know that *Gott* doesn't just grant us every demand we make," Eliza replied, tutting at Patience, who shook her head.

"But all I've prayed for is happiness, Eliza. I've prayed for a husband and my prayers haven't been answered," Patience replied, folding her arms in a sulk.

Ever since she had seen Eliza courting Matthew, her one prayer, every night before bed, as she kneeled in her bedroom, was that *Gott* would send her a husband. She thought she could only be happy again if that one prayer was answered and the more she prayed, the further away she felt from that prayer being answered.

"Oh, Patience, happiness isn't dependent on a man, it's not dependent on anyone or anything but *Gott*. It's *Gott* that gives us happiness, everything else is just grass, burned up in the furnace, fleeting moments. Don't be fooled by the world into thinking you need a husband to be happy," Eliza replied, reaching out and taking Patience by the hand.

"That's easy for you to say. You've got everything you

ever wanted. A husband, a home, a life together. That's all I want, too." Patience said.

Eliza smiled. "Don't set your standards on others, Patience. We all have things we want, things we don't have, dreams unfulfilled. I'll say it again, if you base your happiness on finding a husband, and that alone, then it's no happiness at all. I've told you this before, we all have. Look at Annie, isn't she happy? She's not got a husband, but she's got something precious to her. Where your treasure is, there your heart is, too, that's what the scriptures say. You need to find what really gives you joy. It doesn't have to be a man," Eliza said, as the kettle boiled on the stove.

As Eliza made the drinks, Patience thought about what her sister had said. She had said it before, of course, for this was not the first time that Patience had come to her in distress. But as the months went by, Patience was growing ever more despondent at the prospect of finding the man she dreamed of. She was not willing to settle for just anyone, but it seemed that everyone in Faith's Creek was taken, the hope of finding the right man seemed to be growing fainter day by day.

"But what else is there?" Patience asked.

Eliza tutted. "You could give more service to the church, you could start your own little business or a small holding, you could even help Annie at the schoolhouse. You have too much time on your hands, Patience," Eliza said, just as footsteps on the porch announced the arrival of Matthew.

Patience had always liked him, there was something about his smile that drew her to him, and now he greeted her warmly, sitting down heavily in one of the chairs, as Eliza poured out the coffee.

"Did you get the fence fixed?" she asked.

Matthew nodded. "Those winds we had last week had clean blown it down. It didn't take long to fix it, but Bishop Beiler was pleased. Sarah says she'll bake us a cake to thank us," he said.

Eliza smiled. "We don't need thanking. Bishop Beiler's done more than enough for us," Eliza said, sitting down next to Matthew, and taking a sip of her drink.

"He was saying that the Smithson place is let," Matthew said.

Eliza's eyes widened. "That old place up on the hill

over there?" she exclaimed, gesturing behind her.

Matthew nodded.

Abraham Smithson had been an eccentric, and when he died, his family had wanted nothing to do with Faith's Creek or their strange ways. The house had lain empty for years and was so run down it seemed impossible that anyone would wish to rent it.

"A man named Noah King from Ohio, a widower, and his nephew Caleb. They moved in two days ago. I thought I saw some lights up there the other night, but I assumed it was just kids messing around. Still, they're our neighbors and we'd best make them welcome," Matthew said.

Eliza nodded. "We should invite them for dinner, Matthew, make them feel welcome. You'll come, too, won't you Patience?" she asked.

Read Patience's Faith now FREE with Kindle Unlimited.

Find all Sarah's books on Amazon and click the yellow follow button

This book is dedicated to the wonderful Amish people and the faithful life that they live.

Go in peace my friends.

As an independent author, Sarah relies on your support. If you enjoyed this book, please leave a review on Amazon or Goodreads.

ABOUT THE AUTHOR

Sarah Miller was born in Pennsylvania and spent her childhood close to the Amish people. Weekends were spent doing chores; quilting or eventually babysitting in the community. She grew up to love their culture and the simple lifestyle and had many Amish friends. The one thing that you can guarantee when you are near the Amish, Sarah believes is that you will feel close to God.

Many years later she married Martin who is the love of her life and moved to England. There she started to write stories about the Amish. Recently after a lot of persuasion from her best friend she has decided to publish her stories. They draw on inspiration from her relationship with the Amish and with God and she hopes you enjoy reading them as much as she did writing them. Many of the stories are based on true events but names have been changed and even though they are authentic at times artistic license has been used.

Sarah likes her stories simple and to hold a message and they help bring her closer to her faith. She currently lives in Yorkshire, England with her husband Martin and seven very spoiled chickens.

She would love to meet you on Facebook at https://www.facebook.com/SarahMillerBooks

Sarah hopes her stories will both entertain and inspire and she wishes that you go with God.